The Cousins
Anthony Carrino and John Colaneri
WHAT CAN YOU DO with a TOOLBOX?

Illustrated by **Maple Lam**

A PAULA WISEMAN BOOK
Simon & Schuster Books for Young Readers
New York London Toronto Sydney New Delhi

What's that big red box?

This is a toolbox.

What can you do with a toolbox?

It's what's *inside* a toolbox that is useful. . . .

Do you want to learn what we can do with a toolbox?

Safety always comes first.

These are safety glasses to protect our eyes.

These are hard hats to protect our heads.

Work gloves and boots keep our hands and feet safe.

Now it's time to build!

We build with tools.

And we always use tools with adults.

This is a wrench.

We use a wrench to turn a nut.

We use a wrench and nuts and bolts
to assemble the swing set.

Not all tools fit in a toolbox.

This is a shovel.

We use a shovel to fill the sandbox with sand.

This is a screwdriver.

A screwdriver turns a screw
to fasten the cargo net.

This is a tape measure.

We use it to measure how tall to make the slide.

This is a level.

We use it to make sure the monkey bars are straight.

This is a hammer.

Those are nails.

We use a hammer and nails to connect floorboards when we build a deck.

This is a saw.

We use a saw to cut the railing for stairs.

This is a drill.

We use a drill to tighten the screws and bolts to assemble the doorframe.

This is a ladder.

We use a ladder to reach the roof.

These are paintbrushes.

With paintbrushes and paint we can turn the walls any color we want!

What can we do with a toolbox?

We can build

a playground!

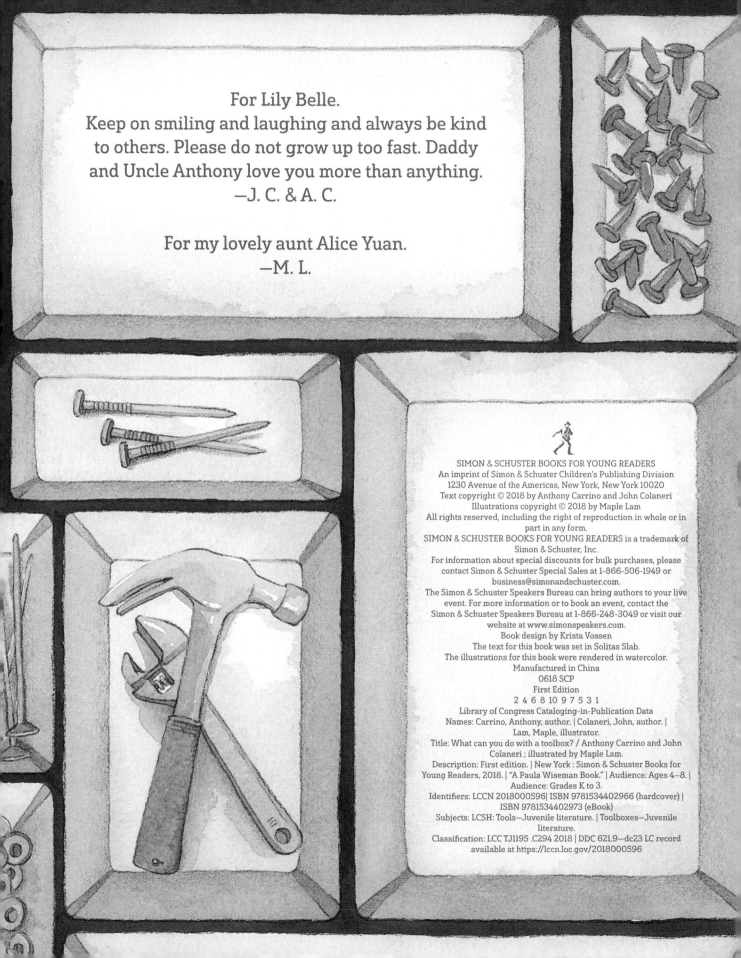

For Lily Belle.
Keep on smiling and laughing and always be kind
to others. Please do not grow up too fast. Daddy
and Uncle Anthony love you more than anything.
—J. C. & A. C.

For my lovely aunt Alice Yuan.
—M. L.

SIMON & SCHUSTER BOOKS FOR YOUNG READERS
An imprint of Simon & Schuster Children's Publishing Division
1230 Avenue of the Americas, New York, New York 10020
Text copyright © 2018 by Anthony Carrino and John Colaneri
Illustrations copyright © 2018 by Maple Lam
All rights reserved, including the right of reproduction in whole or in
part in any form.
SIMON & SCHUSTER BOOKS FOR YOUNG READERS is a trademark of
Simon & Schuster, Inc.
For information about special discounts for bulk purchases, please
contact Simon & Schuster Special Sales at 1-866-506-1949 or
business@simonandschuster.com.
The Simon & Schuster Speakers Bureau can bring authors to your live
event. For more information or to book an event, contact the
Simon & Schuster Speakers Bureau at 1-866-248-3049 or visit our
website at www.simonspeakers.com.
Book design by Krista Vossen
The text for this book was set in Solitas Slab.
The illustrations for this book were rendered in watercolor.
Manufactured in China
0618 SCP
First Edition
2 4 6 8 10 9 7 5 3 1
Library of Congress Cataloging-in-Publication Data
Names: Carrino, Anthony, author. | Colaneri, John, author. |
Lam, Maple, illustrator.
Title: What can you do with a toolbox? / Anthony Carrino and John
Colaneri ; illustrated by Maple Lam.
Description: First edition. | New York : Simon & Schuster Books for
Young Readers, 2018. | "A Paula Wiseman Book." | Audience: Ages 4–8. |
Audience: Grades K to 3.
Identifiers: LCCN 2018000596| ISBN 9781534402966 (hardcover) |
ISBN 9781534402973 (eBook)
Subjects: LCSH: Tools—Juvenile literature. | Toolboxes—Juvenile
literature.
Classification: LCC TJ1195 .C294 2018 | DDC 621.9—dc23 LC record
available at https://lccn.loc.gov/2018000596